IMAGINE

An Inspirational Story of Calming Strategies for Children

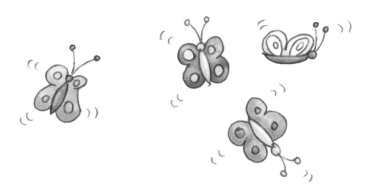

Written By Elisa Holton Odegard
Illustrated By CA Nobens

Liam,
May all of
your days
be filled
with joy and
imagination!
♡, Elisa
Holton
Odegard

Dedicated to all of my precious students, especially Jon Butler, for inspiring me to never give up reaching for my dreams!

Also dedicated to my dear family, whose continuous love and support means the world to me! I love you!

Elisa Holton Odegard

Edited by Alicia Ester
Illustrated by CA Nobens
Cover and interior design by CA Nobens

ISBN: 978-1-64343-888-7
First Printing: 2020
Library of Congress Catalog Number: 2020907833
24 23 22 21 20 5 4 3 2 1
Printed in Canada

BEAVER'S POND
PRESS

Beaver's Pond Press, Inc.
939 Seventh Street West,
Saint Paul, MN 55102

(952) 829-8818   www.BeaversPondPress.com

Visit www.handprintonmyheart.org for resources to help children with anxiety and mental health issues, and to contact the author about school visits and interviews.

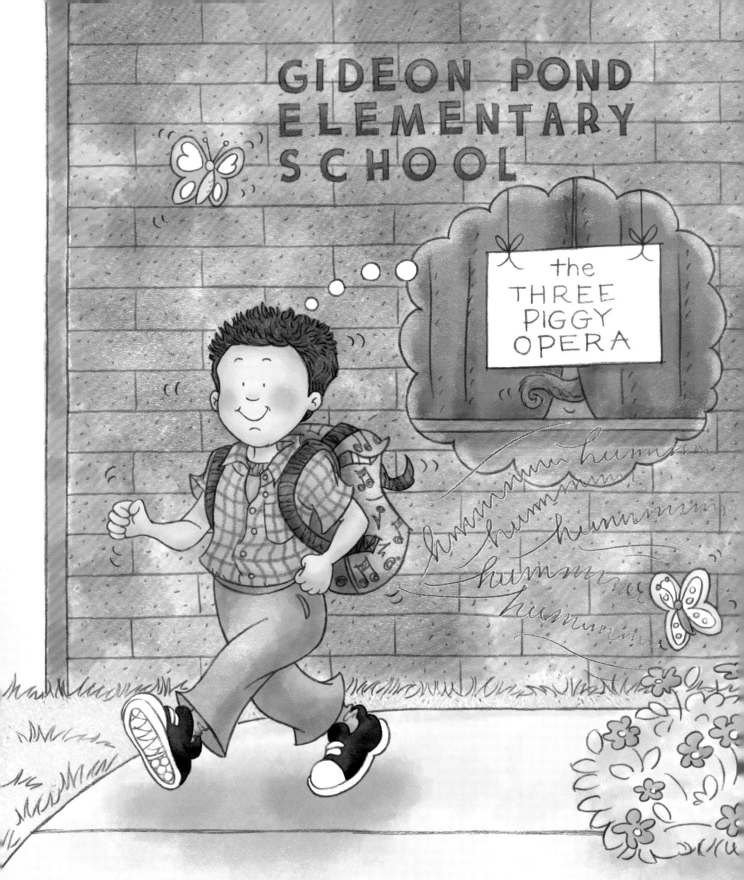

Jon hummed all the way to school, as he knew it was going to be a wonderful day! Today his class was practicing their musical play. Oh, how Jon loved to sing, dance, and act! He knew that with a lot of work, he could be anything he wanted to be. He was excited to be cast as the Big Bad Wolf in *The Three Piggy Opera*. But Jon was not a big, bad person. He was kind. He would have to IMAGINE how to be the wolf.

In the hallway, Jon was still thinking about acting. Words in the script would make pictures in his head and help him move his body like the wolf.

He heard Matthew grumble, "Some boy knocked my backpack off my hook and walked away." A concerned Jon said, "Maybe he had a hard morning. He probably didn't mean to do it."

But Matthew was still upset. Jon wondered if acting would help his friend feel better. He tried to think of something cheerful.

"Try this," suggested Jon. "Press your hands to either side of your face and take big breaths. Then IMAGINE you are watching your favorite animal at the zoo."

Matthew took the advice of his caring friend and pictured himself at the monkey habitat, beginning his day with a happier mindset.

In the classroom, Najma had trouble starting her morning work. "How can I do my best job if someone took my pencil?" She looked around but couldn't guess who had done it.

"You are smart. I know you can solve this without getting mad," offered Jon. But Najma still seemed tense.

Jon continued, "Take a deep breath. Hold yourself up off of your chair. IMAGINE you are a gymnast on a balance beam."

Najma acted it out. A smile came across her face, as it healed her heart! Then she hopped over to the writing toolbox to borrow a pencil.

Later that morning, Jon and his classmates worked on writing. Ashley gave him a look of despair. "I don't know what to write because someone was talking during our teacher's directions!" she exclaimed.

Jon thought about how a director would encourage an actor. He explained the assignment, then said, "You can do it, Ashley! Take a deep breath, stretching your arms straight above your head. IMAGINE that you are diving into a cool swimming pool."

IMAGINE IMAGINE IMAGINE

Ashley loved to swim. How sweet of Jon to remember! It made her feel relaxed, so she gratefully got busy.

At literacy center time, Jon saw a tear fall down Caitlin's face. "This book is really hard to read," she worried out loud.

Jon kindly gave her an elbow nudge and said, "I think you are a good reader." However, Caitlin still had doubts.

"Give this a try," guided Jon. "First, take a breath. Then push the palms of your hands together strongly, with your fingers resting on opposite wrists. Now IMAGINE you are reading like a royal queen."

Caitlin gleefully tried what Jon said and found her royal voice to remind her to believe in herself.

Soon it was time to line up for recess. "Why do some people have to cut in front of me?" questioned Ibrahim.

"Don't pay attention to them," Jon gently advised. "Dip your chin to your chest and swing your head shoulder to shoulder. IMAGINE you are on a swing at the playground already."

GINE IMAGINE

Ibrahim could hardly contain his snickering as he tried it. The student who had cut in front of him joined in and gave Ibrahim his spot back.

Once they were outside, Jon saw Marcos fall. "I was playing four square and somebody bumped me to the ground," complained Marcos.

Jon helped him up and gave an important tip. "Accidents happen. Think of a song you love and make your fingers pretend to play it on a piano. IMAGINE you're playing a solo on the stage of a grand concert hall."

Marcos moved slowly at first but tried it. Soon he was playing four square again, hearing joyful music in his head.

Lunchtime followed. "What's wrong?" Jon asked. "I get headaches from all the shouting in the cafeteria," EmJae explained.

Jon whispered in her ear, "How about this? Fill your lungs with air. Face a wall and push forward and backward several times. Then IMAGINE you are shaking a piñata filled with candy!"

EmJae used a wall to do the strategy while picturing the colorful piñata. Now the lunchroom chatter sounded like students cheering her on. To her surprise, she found peace and enjoyed her lunch.

During a math activity that afternoon, Trang was upset. "I can't find the counting cubes that I am supposed to use anywhere!"

"Try not to get worried," said Jon. "Instead, spread out your five fingers on one hand and blow on each one. Then IMAGINE they are dandelions with their seeds floating away in a summer field."

IMAGINE IMD

Trang shut his eyes as he visualized such a wonderful thought. He opened them and cooperated with his partner to find the hidden cubes.

Near the end of the day, the teacher clapped her hands. "It's time to practice *The Three Piggy Opera!*" she announced. Jon loved acting and singing most of all!

He was so excited to rehearse that he skipped too quickly to his place. He tripped and landed sprawled out on the floor.

The class laughed uproariously!

Jon awkwardly stood up with his head hung low. The class stopped laughing. They could see that Jon was deeply embarrassed.

Eight students immediately scampered up to him, offering their new calming strategies from that day, hoping to help Jon get over his hurt feelings as he had helped them.

Jon and his friends giggled at the overwhelming response of friendship!

"IMAGINE what our classroom community would feel like if we all found ways to stay calm and think of our friends' feelings before our own," said the teacher. "I no longer have to IMAGINE it," she proclaimed proudly. "You just did it together!"

Humming all the way, Jon headed home with a grin. His friends could have acted like big bad wolves when they were upset. Instead, thoughtful acts of kindness turned the day into pictures of happiness and words of gratitude. It was music to his ears! He couldn't IMAGINE it any other way!

IMAGINE

Calming Strategies for Children with Anxiety

Take deep, calming breaths to enhance the following strategies. You can make any decision that works best for you. You may want to try coping in a quiet location away from the stressful area, with permission. You might feel better staying in the same place. Repeat these calming ideas, as needed, until you have returned to being focused.

"At the Zoo" = Press your hands to either side of your face, fingertips on your temples.

"Gymnastics Practice" = As you sit in a chair, push your hands into your seat near your legs and push your body off the chair, while keeping your legs straight out in front of you. Try to hold yourself up.

"Swimmer's Dive" = Stretch your arms straight up above your head and lean your body to one side.

"Royal Pose" = Push the palms of your hands together strongly, with your fingers resting on opposite wrists and your posture straight.

"Playground Swing" = Dip your chin to your chest and swing your head shoulder to shoulder, forward only.

"Piano Player" = Think of your favorite song in your head, while your fingers pretend to play a piano in the air in front of your stomach.

"Piñata Shake" = Stand facing a wall and push forward and backward on it, at shoulder level, several times (similar to a standing push-up).

"Dandelion Wish" = Spread out your five fingers on one hand and blow on each one.

IMAGINE: Vocabulary Study

1. Imagine ~ To form a picture in your head of an idea, commonly positive

2. Script ~ The written words of a play that tell the actors what to say and do

3. Grumble ~ To complain about something with a low rumbling sound

4. Mindset ~ The attitude someone holds in their mind about a situation

5. Despair ~ Feeling the complete loss of hope

6. Gratitude ~ Being thankful, showing appreciation for kindness

7. Nudge ~ To gently touch someone, typically with an elbow, to encourage them to do something

8. Royal ~ Having the special title of a king or queen or being a member of their family

9. Snicker ~ To half-laugh

10. Piñata ~ A decorated 3-D figure, typically an animal, containing toys and candy that hangs from a string so that blindfolded children can break it open with a stick as part of a traditional Spanish-speaking celebration

11. Strategy ~ A plan put into place to meet a major goal

12. Dandelion ~ A weed, in the daisy family, with bright yellow flowers that turn into fluffy tufts with seeds

13. Visualize ~ To see a picture in your mind from words described to you

14. Uproarious ~ Loud laughter from something very funny

IMAGINE

When feeling frustrated or upset, use a calming strategy and IMAGINE yourself somewhere fun or exciting!

Draw yourself doing one of your favorite strategies from the story or create one of your own.

Then share it with a friend!

About the Author & Illustrator:

Elisa Odegard has been teaching elementary school for twenty-eight years, primarily kindergarten and first grade. Her passion is to inspire children to love reading for learning and enjoyment, as well as supporting their social and emotional needs. This is her first published children's book, a lifelong dream come true. A proud Minnesotan all her life, she lives there with her devoted husband, Lance, and two endearing children, Ashley and Matthew. She is so grateful for God's many blessings in her life, including her special students.

CA Nobens has been writing, illustrating, and designing books for children for about forty years. She lives and works in Saint Louis Park, Minnesota in a ninety-year-old house, with people and cats (numbers vary).